# Classic Fairy Tales
adapted by
# Christine Deverell

©2002  Grandreams Books Limited.

Published by Grandreams Books Ltd,
4 North Parade, Bath, BA1 1LF, UK.

Grandreams Books Inc.,
360 Hurst Street, Linden, NJ  07036 USA

Printed in China.

# · C O N T E N T S ·

**The Three Little Pigs**    4

**Cinderella**    16

**The Ugly Duckling**    26

**Beauty and the Beast**    38

**The Wolf and the Seven Little Goats**    50

**Old Mother Frost**    59

**The King's New Clothes**    71

**Rapunzel**    81

# The Three Little Pigs

ILLUSTRATED BY KATE DAVIES

Once upon a time there were three little pigs, and one summer's day they decided to go out into the big, wide world on their own. As they walked along a forest path they talked about what they would do. "We will each need to find a plot and build ourselves a house to live in," said one little pig to his brothers.

They passed a man with a cart piled high with straw. The first little pig asked the man if he could have some straw to

build himself a house. The man was glad to give him straw, and the little pig waved goodbye to the other two, built a house and was very pleased with himself.

Soon, an old grey wolf came by, and when he saw the straw house he stopped and looked through the window.

Inside he saw the little pig. So he went to the door, knocked gently and said,

in his sweetest voice,

"Little pig, little pig, can I come in?"

And the little pig answered,

"No, not by the hair of my chinny, chin, chin."

"Then I'll huff, and I'll puff, and I'll blow your house down." growled the wolf.

And he huffed, and he puffed, and he blew the house down, and ate up the little pig.

Meanwhile the other little pigs walked on, until they met a man carrying a cartload of twigs. One of the little pigs said

to the man, "Would you give me some of these twigs to build a house?" And the man was glad to give him the twigs. The little pig waved goodbye to his friend, built a house and was very pleased with himself.

Soon, the old grey wolf came by, and when he saw the twig house he stopped and looked through the window. Inside he saw the second little pig. So he went to the door, knocked gently and said, in his sweetest voice, "Little pig, little pig, can I come in?" And the little pig answered, "No, not by the

hair of my chinny, chin, chin."

"Then I'll huff, and I'll puff, and I'll blow your house down," growled the wolf.

And he huffed, and he puffed, and he blew the house down, and ate up the little pig.

Now the third little pig was much smarter than the other two. He saw a man with a cartload of bricks, and he thought,

"This is just what I need."

So he begged the man to let him have enough bricks to build himself a house, and the man was happy to give him as many as he wanted. So the little pig built himself a fine brick house with a kitchen and a big fireplace.

Along came the wolf who knocked on the door and said,

"Little pig, little pig, can I come in?"
And the little pig answered,

"No, not by the hair of my chinny, chin, chin."

"Then I'll huff, and I'll puff, and I'll blow your house down." growled the wolf.

And he huffed, and he puffed, and he huffed, and he puffed, but no matter how hard he huffed and puffed, the wolf could not blow the house down. The little pig laughed at the wolf through the window. The wolf made a plan.

9

"If I want to eat this pig," he said to himself, "then I will have to trick him." So he called, "Little pig, little pig, I know where there is a lovely field of turnips."

"Where?" asked the little pig.

"Behind farmer Smith's house; and if you are ready at six o'clock tomorrow morning, I will call for you, and we can go together."

"Very well. I will be ready," said the little pig. But the little pig got up at five o'clock, ran to farmer Smith's field, filled a sack with turnips and was safely back in his house when the wolf called for him at six.

"Are you ready, little pig?" called the wolf.

"Ha, ha!" laughed the pig, "I thought you said to be ready at five. I have already been to the turnip field and now I am making a stew for my dinner."

The wolf was very angry, but in a sweet, gentle voice he said,

"Little pig, there is a fine apple orchard at Oakwood Farm. Be ready at five tomorrow and we will go together."

"Very well," said the little pig, "I'll see you tomorrow."

But the little pig got up at four and made his own way to the apple orchard. He climbed a tree to fill his sack, and just as he was about to come down, he saw the wolf approaching. The wolf called up to him,

"Ah, little pig, you did not wait for me. Are they nice apples?"

"Yes, absolutely delicious; I will throw one to you," said the pig.

He threw it as far as he could, so that as the wolf ran to catch it, the little pig jumped down from the tree and ran home as fast as he could.

The next day the wolf knocked at the little pig's door and said, "There is a fair in the town this afternoon, will you be going?"

"Oh yes," said the little pig excitedly, "I love going to the fair; what time will you be ready?"

"At three o'clock," said the wolf. As usual, the little pig left home early and made his way to the fair alone. He bought himself a butter churn, and was on his way home with it when he saw the wolf coming along the road towards him.

He quickly climbed into the butter churn, and set it rolling down the hill and heading straight for the wolf. The wolf was so frightened that he turned tail and ran all the way home again.

Later that evening the wolf went to the little pig's house. He stood at the door telling his sad tale of how frightened he had been at the sight of a butter churn coming at him at great speed.

Then the little pig laughed at him and said, "That was me inside the butter churn!"

This made the wolf very angry indeed, and he growled,

"I will eat you up, I will, I will. I am going to come down the chimney to get you!"

As the wolf climbed up onto the roof the little pig stoked up the fire in the huge fireplace, and put a pot of water on to boil.

The wolf fell down the chimney and landed in the pot,
and the little pig boiled him up and ate him for supper. The
little pig lived safely and happily in his brick house for many
years.

# Cinderella

## ILLUSTRATED BY BRIAN ROBERTSON

Once upon a time a rich gentleman who was sad after the death of his wife, decided to marry again, so his lovely daughter could have a mother to care for her. Unfortunately he chose a proud and selfish woman with two daughters just like herself. She did not reveal her true

character until after the wedding. She ordered the little girl to work in the kitchen and live with the servants, while she and her daughters enjoyed a life of splendour.

When the child had finished her work, she used to sit in the chimney corner among the cinders; so everyone called her Cinderella. Her clothes were dirty and ragged, but she was far prettier than her sisters in all their fine clothes.

One day an invitation arrived from the palace. The King's son was giving a ball! The sisters could not have been happier. They talked of nothing but what they would wear, and ordered beautiful gowns from the best dressmakers in the land.

Cinderella would have loved to go to the ball, and the wicked sisters teased her mercilessly saying;

"Wouldn't you just love to dress up in these fine clothes and ride in a carriage to the palace, and dance with rich young men, and maybe even with the Prince himself?"

It was known that the Prince was in search of a wife, and Cinderella's mean stepmother had high hopes for her daughters. Soon, the great day arrived. Cinderella was busy all day, dressing her sisters, polishing their shoes, combing their hair, and when the splendid carriage arrived to take them to the ball, she dutifully arranged their gowns so they would not crumple on the journey.

When they were out of sight, Cinderella sat down alone and exhausted in the chimney corner and began to cry. Then, all of a sudden, her Fairy Godmother appeared and said,

"Why are you crying?"

"I wish I could go to the ball," sobbed Cinderella.

"Well then, be a good girl and do as I say. And you shall go to the ball! Run along to the garden and bring me a pumpkin."

Cinderella found the biggest and best pumpkin and brought it to her Fairy Godmother who touched it with her magic wand. Instantly it became a beautiful golden coach.

"Now bring me the mouse-trap, and open it very carefully."

Six mice ran out of the trap, and as the Fairy Godmother touched each one with her wand, it turned into a fine dapple grey horse. Cinderella was then sent to find a rat for her Fairy Godmother to turn into a handsome postilion, and six lizards which became smart footmen.

19

"Well now, will that be fit to carry a lady to the ball?" asked the Fairy Godmother.

"Oh yes. It's wonderful," replied Cinderella, "but . . ."

"Aha! You're wondering what you are going to wear, are you not? Let's see; what would suit you?"

With these words, she waved her wand over Cinderella, and in an instant her rags became the most magnificent dress you can imagine. She was wearing the most costly jewels in the world, and on her feet was a beautiful pair of glass slippers. "Off you go now," said the Fairy Godmother, "but mind you leave the palace before the clock strikes twelve, or all this magic will be undone."

Cinderella promised to obey, and set off in her golden carriage. When she appeared in the ballroom, everyone fell silent and the music and dancing stopped, for she was the most beautiful young woman in the room. The young Prince took her hand and led her out to dance with him. He danced with no one else the whole evening.

When they sat down to the feast, he was so busy looking at her that he did not eat a thing! The dancing continued. Cinderella was so happy, she had danced every dance and did

not feel tired. Then she heard a clock striking the hour.

"It must be 11 o'clock. It cannot possibly be midnight yet," she said to herself, mindful of her Fairy Godmother's warning.

But as she turned and saw the clock, Cinderella gasped with fright and ran as fast as she could from the ballroom. The Prince tried to catch up with her as the clock continued to chime.

As she ran through the door and down the steps towards the golden carriage, she lost one of her glass slippers, and at

the very moment that the Prince bent down to retrieve it, the clock struck twelve. As he stood up, the Prince did not see a sign of his beautiful dancing partner; and the coach and horses had completely vanished. Behind a hedge in the garden sat poor Cinderella in her ragged, dirty clothes.

Beside her was the pumpkin; and the mice, the rat and the lizards scurried away. When she was certain that the Prince

had gone, Cinderella made her way home on foot as fast as she could. The music and dancing would have continued until morning, but the Prince was in no mood for celebration, and all the guests were sent away. He took the glass slipper to the King and said,

"I will find the maiden whose foot this slipper fits, and when I have found her, she will be my bride."

Cinderella's stepmother grew very excited when the Prince arrived at their house.

"It's only a shoe," she said to her daughters; "one of you will be able to squeeze your foot into it." But they tried in vain. It was a tiny, dainty slipper, and the sisters had big, clumsy feet.

"Are there any other young women in this house?" asked the Prince.

"Only Cinderella," said the mother, "but she works in the kitchen, and we didn't take her to the ball."

"Bring her here," demanded the Prince. And when Cinderella

tried on the slipper everyone cried,

"It fits! It fits!" The stepmother and her daughters were white with rage.

The Prince looked into Cinderella's eyes and recognised that she was indeed the beautiful stranger he had danced with, and he took her away to be his bride. They lived happily for many years in the great palace, and the Princess, who later became Queen, was always kind to her servants, and invited them to attend the annual ball.

# The Ugly Duckling

ILLUSTRATED BY KEN OLIVER

It was summertime, and it was beautiful in the country. The sunshine fell warmly on an old house surrounded by deep canals. From the wall around the house to the edge of the water there grew large burdock leaves, so high that children could hide in them, and it was here that a duck had built her nest and laid her eggs. She was growing very tired of sitting on her eggs when at last she heard a crack.

One little head popped out, then another, and then another. They waddled out to the edge of the leaves and peeped out.

"The world is so big!" they said to their mother.

She counted the ducklings and checked the nest, and there was one egg, the largest, that lay unhatched.

The mother duck sat on the egg until at last it cracked open, and out tumbled the largest and ugliest duckling she had ever seen.

"That is a big, strong creature," she said, "not at all like the others."

The next day the sun was shining warmly when the mother duck and her family went down to the canal. Splash! she went into the water, and called to the ducklings to follow. One by one they jumped in, and they swam quite easily.

Even the ugly grey one was swimming around with the rest of them.

"Quack, quack!" said the mother duck.

"Come with me now, and I will show you the world; but keep close to me or someone may tread on you, and watch out for the cat."

They came to the duckyard, where other duck families were gathered.

"You must bow to the old duck that you see over there," said the mother duck, "for she is nobly born and of Spanish blood."

The other ducks in the yard stared at the new brood, and then began to talk to each other;

"Look how ugly that one is!" they said, and one of the ducks flew at him and bit his neck.

"Leave him alone," said his mother, "he is not doing any harm."

"Those are fine children that you have," said the old

duck, "they are all very pretty except for that one."

"Certainly, he is not handsome," said the mother, "but he is very good and he can swim as well as the others, indeed rather better."

She stroked the Ugly Duckling's neck with her beak and smoothed his ruffled feathers. The day did not go well for the poor Ugly Duckling. He was bitten, pecked and teased by both ducks and hens and the turkeys terrified him.

Things got much worse as the days went by; the girl who fed the poultry kicked him, and even his own brothers and sisters were unkind to him. He decided to run away. He ran through the hedge, and the little sparrows were frightened

and flew away. "That is because I am so ugly," he thought, and ran on. He came to a moor where some wild ducks lived.

"You are really very ugly,' said the wild ducks to their new companion,

"but that does not matter to us, as long as you do not wish to marry into our family."

Poor thing! He had no thought of marrying. All he wanted was to live among the reeds and drink the water on the moor. He was happy there for two days, but on the third day he awoke to the sound of guns and barking dogs, and the sight of ducks and geese falling from the sky.

He kept very still as the dogs splashed about in the mud, bending the reeds and rushes in all directions. For one terrifying moment, a fierce looking dog thrust his nose into the duckling's face, and then ran off.

"Well!" said he to himself, "I am so ugly that even a dog does not want to look at me."

It was late in the afternoon before silence fell, and the Ugly Duckling waited another hour before he ran away

as fast as he could from the moor. As it grew dark he reached a little hut, and when he saw that the door was broken, leaving a hole big enough for him to get through, he crept inside.

In this one roomed hut there lived an old woman with her cat who sat on her lap and purred contentedly, and a hen who laid good eggs.

They were all asleep and did not notice their visitor until the morning. The cat mewed and the hen began to cackle.

"What's the matter?" asked the old woman, looking round. Her eyes were not good, and she took the duckling to be a fat duck who had got lost.

"If this is not a drake, we might have duck's eggs as well as hen's eggs."

For three weeks the duckling sat in a corner of the hut feeling very sad.

31

One day the old woman opened the door and he felt the bright sunshine on his feathers. This gave him such a yearning to swim that he could not help but tell the hen.

"What is the matter with you?" said the hen.

"You have nothing to do all day, so you sit here dreaming. Why don't you lay eggs, or purr, and forget these fantasies?"

"Oh, but it is so delicious to swim," said the duckling, "so delicious when the waters close over your head and you plunge to the bottom."

"I think you must be crazy," said the hen, "why don't you ask the cat - he is the wisest creature I know - whether he would like to swim, or to plunge to the bottom of the water. Or ask your mistress. No one is cleverer than she. Do you think she would take pleasure in swimming, and in the waters closing over her head?"

"You do not understand me," sobbed the Ugly Duckling.

"What! do you think yourself wiser than the cat and the old woman, not to mention myself? You ought to be grateful for all the kindness that has been shown to you here. Do you not have a warm room to live in? And are you not lucky to have our company and the benefit of our wisdom and experience? Believe me, I want you to be happy. I know I tell you unpleasant truths, but this is what friends are for. Come on, do yourself a favour and learn to purr or to lay eggs."

"I think I will take my chance, and go out into the wide world again," said the duckling.

33

"Well, off you go then," said the hen, and he escaped through the open door. He soon found water, and swam on the surface and plunged to the bottom. But all the other animals ignored him:

"It's because I am so ugly," he said to himself.

Autumn came, and the leaves turned yellow and brown. The poor little Ugly Duckling began to shiver as the air grew colder. One evening, just as the sun was setting, a flock of large birds took to the sky. They were the most beautiful creatures the duckling had ever seen; their feathers were white, and their necks were long and slender. They were swans, and they flew away to warmer climes.

It was a cold, cold winter, and the poor little duckling felt so alone. He very nearly froze to death in the ice, when a peasant noticed him, picked him up and took him home to his wife and children. He soon revived, and the children wanted to play with him, but he was afraid of them, and ran away into the snow again.

It would be just too sad to tell you all the things that happened to him that winter. He was lying beside the canal among some reeds one day when he felt the warmth of the sun on his feathers. The larks were singing and spring had returned. The Ugly Duckling came out into the sunshine and shook his wings. They were stronger than before, and he flew, close to the water, until he landed in a garden with apple trees in full blossom. The sights and the smells were delightful.

Three beautiful swans came swimming proudly along the canal. The duckling was so excited when he saw them that he flew into the water and swam towards them.

"They will probably ignore me, for I am so ugly," he thought, and he hung his head in shame. As he did so, he

caught sight of his reflection in the water. And what he saw before him was not a plump, ugly, grey bird, but a beautiful, white swan!

The larger swans swam around him and stroked his neck with their beaks, and he was very happy. He remembered how he had been laughed at and cruelly treated, and now he heard everyone say that he was the most beautiful of all birds. He said to himself,

"How little did I dream of so much happiness when I was the ugly, despised duckling!"

# Beauty and the Beast

## ILLUSTRATED BY DAVID LONG

Once upon a time there was a merchant who had three beautiful daughters. The eldest sisters cared only for fine dresses and jewels, but the youngest, called Beauty, had a kind and gentle heart, and was especially loved by her father. One day, the merchant was going off on a long journey, and he asked his daughters what they would like him to bring home.

"I'd like a fine, emerald necklace," said the eldest.

"And a pearl necklace for me," cried the second.

"I would like you to bring yourself home as soon as possible," said Beauty, "and if you can find one, I would like a white rose."

The two sisters made fun of Beauty for asking their father to bring her a rose.

"You have lots of roses in your garden," they said.

"But I do not have a white one," said Beauty, and she wondered why they wanted jewels. The merchant did not forget his daughters' wishes, and before returning home he bought an emerald necklace and a pearl necklace.

But nowhere could he find a white rose for Beauty, for it

was winter, and snow was falling. As he was nearing home, the merchant missed his way in the snowstorm, and could not tell where he was. Just as he was about to turn round, he saw lights ahead, and soon found himself at the door of a great castle.

He hoped that they would offer him shelter for the night, and as he went to knock on the door, he saw that it was open.

Not a servant was in sight, so he went inside. In the great hall, he found a splendid supper laid out. He sat down and enjoyed the feast. In the corner of the hall was an open door,

and when he looked in, he saw a bedroom that looked as if it had been prepared for him.

The merchant was very tired, so he went to bed and slept soundly. In the morning a fine suit had been laid out for him to wear, and a hearty breakfast awaited him in the hall. He would have liked to thank his kind host, but still the merchant saw no one. As he walked through the garden on his way to the stable to collect his horse, he spied a beautiful rose bush covered with white blooms.

Thinking of his daughter and her request, he reached out and picked a single rose. Suddenly a terrible roar sounded from the bushes and a huge, ugly beast sprang out.

"Who is stealing my white rose?" he growled.
The poor merchant trembled and could barely speak.

"I did not mean to steal. "My daughter begged me to bring

her a white rose and this is the only one I have seen."

"It is my favourite rose, and anyone who touches it must die!" said the Beast,

"But I will let you go if you promise to bring me the first thing that runs to meet you when you get home."

The merchant agreed, and as he made his journey home, he hoped that it might be the cat that came out to meet him, and not his beloved dog.

But as he approached the house, it was his little daughter Beauty who came running towards him. He turned so pale that when she saw her father, Beauty thought he must be very sick. He gave her the white rose and took her hand. He told her all that had happened to him and the promise he had made to the Beast.

"But I will never, never give you up Beauty," he said.

"You must keep your promise, Father," said Beauty,

"perhaps he will not hurt me."

So they prepared to return to the castle. They rode silently through the forest, for they were too sad to speak. At the castle they found the front door open and a meal laid out in the great hall, only this time the table was set for two. They sat down, but Beauty and her father could not eat.

Then, at nine o'clock, they heard a great roar and the Beast appeared.

He spoke gently to them, saying to the merchant,

"You may stay here tonight, but tomorrow you must go home and leave Beauty behind. Do not worry about her; she will have all she could wish for here."

Father and daughter parted with great sadness. But Beauty soon became quite contented with her life in the castle. Her room was very pretty, with roses outside her window, and on a table stood a wonderful mirror. In golden letters around

the outside was written, "See your wishes, here enshrined, What you long for, you will find."

"I will be able to wish myself home whenever I am unhappy," said Beauty to herself. And she often looked into the mirror to see what was happening to her father and sisters at home, for she spent every day amusing herself, and saw no one until the evening when the Beast joined her for supper.

After they had eaten Beauty would sing to the Beast. One night he asked her,

"Do you think I am very ugly?" His voice sounded so sad that Beauty found it hard to answer him.

"You have a very kind face," she said at last with a sigh, "but you really are very ugly."

A single tear ran down the Beast's cheek, and Beauty felt so sorry for him.

"I do like you very much," she assured him.

"Then will you marry me, Beauty?"

"O, no! I could never marry a beast," sobbed Beauty. She

went to bed very sad, and looking into the magic mirror she asked to see her family again. The mirror painted a picture of her old home, and in the corner Beauty saw her dear father lying ill in bed.

Next day Beauty could neither play nor work, and could only wait until supper-time came when she could ask the Beast if he would let her go home for just one week to visit her father."

If you go you will never come back to me," said the Beast.

"I promise you I will come back in a week, dear Beast. Let me go," pleaded Beauty.

"Very well," he said, "but take this ring with you, and if you ever want to come back, put it on your finger when you go to bed, and in the morning you will find yourself here in your own room."

That night Beauty looked into the magic mirror and wished herself home. She fell asleep on her bed tightly clutching the ring, and when she woke she was in her father's house. He wept with joy to see his little Beauty again, and began to get well. At the end of one week, Beauty could not bear to leave her father, so she broke her promise to the Beast and stayed another week.

One night, she had a strange dream. She dreamed that she

was back in the Beast's garden, wandering about. As she came to the white rose bush she found the poor Beast lying on the ground, and he looked as if he were dying. As she ran towards him he cried out,

"Oh Beauty, you have broken my heart, and I shall die without you." Beauty woke up from her dream and so longed to see her dear Beast again that she reached out for the magic ring and slipped it onto her finger.

When she next awoke, she found herself back in her pretty room in the Beast's castle, just as he had told her she would.

Remembering her dream, Beauty quickly ran out into the garden to see if he was there. When she reached the white rose bush she found the Beast lying so stiff and quiet that she thought he was dead.

"Oh my dear Beast," cried Beauty as she threw her arms around his neck. "Please don't die, for I have come back to take care of you, and I will marry you, for I love you with all my heart." She put her head in her hands and wept, and when

she stood up, she could not see the Beast. Instead, through the tears, she could only see a handsome young Prince beside her. "Who are you? And what have you done with my Beast?" asked Beauty.

"Do you not know me, dear Beauty?" said the Prince.

"I am the Beast you loved and to whom you gave life and happiness. A witch cast an evil spell over me so that I took the form of an ugly beast, and nothing could set me free until a beautiful girl loved me and promised to marry me."

"If you really are my dear Beast, then I will marry you," said Beauty. Together they went to the magic mirror, and when Beauty looked in she saw her father living for the rest of his days in the castle with her. When the Prince looked in the mirror he saw a wedding, with Beauty his bride carrying a bouquet of white roses. Their wishes came true, and they lived happily ever after.

# The Wolf and the Seven Little Goats

ILLUSTRATED BY KATE DAVIES

Once upon a time there lived a Nanny Goat who had seven young kids. She loved them as any mother loves her children. One day, she wanted to go into the forest, so she called the little goats together and said, "Dear children, I am going away into the wood; be on your guard against the wolf. If he comes here, he will eat you all up.

He may try to fool you into thinking he is someone else, but you will know him by his gruff voice and his black feet."

"Don't worry, mother," the little goats replied, "we'll remember."

So she went on her way, quite happily. Not long after the mother goat had gone, there was a knock at the door and a voice called out,

"Open the door, children; your mother is here and has brought something for each of you."

But the little goats knew from the gruff voice that it was the wolf, so they said,

"No, you cannot come in, you are not our mother. She has

a kind and gentle voice, but yours is gruff; you are a wolf."

So the wolf went home and found a piece of chalk, which he ate. This made his voice more gentle, so he returned to the goats' house, knocked at the door and called out,

"Open, my dear children; your mother has come home and brought you each something."

But the wolf had placed his paws on the window sill. When the little goats saw them they said,

"No, no, we will not open the door to you. Our mother has white paws, and yours are black. You are a wolf."

So the wolf went to a baker and said,

"I have hurt my foot, put some dough on it."

When the baker had done this, the wolf ran to the miller saying,

"Put some white flour on my feet."

But the miller, thinking the wolf was planning to fool someone, refused. But then the wolf said to him,

"If you do not do what I ask, I will eat you."

The miller was afraid, and powdered the wolf's feet with flour. Now, the wicked wolf went for a third time to the goats' house and knocked on the door.

"Open up to me dear children; your mother is come, and I have brought you something nice from the forest."

He put his paws up on the window sill, and when the little goats saw that they were white, they thought it was safe, and they undid the door.

Then who should come in but the wolf! They were so frightened, they ran and hid themselves. One ran under the table, the second crawled under the bed, the third hid in the cupboard, the fourth behind the kitchen door, the fifth in the oven, the sixth in the wash tub and the seventh in the big grandfather clock.

The wolf found them out, and quickly swallowed them up, one after the other; the only little goat he did not discover was in the grandfather clock.

The wolf could hardly move, but dragged himself into the forest, where he lay down to sleep. Soon the little goats'

mother came home. What a terrible sight greeted her. The door was wide open; the table, stools and benches were overturned, the wash tub was broken in pieces, and the sheets were pulled off the bed. She could not find her children anywhere.

She called them all by name, but they did not appear, until she came to the name of the youngest:

"Here I am, mother, in the grandfather clock."

55

When the little one came out, she told her mother what the wolf had done, and they hugged each other and cried. They went out for a walk in the forest, and they came to a glade where they found the wolf sleeping.

The mother goat walked right round the wolf as he lay there snoring, and she thought she saw something moving inside him.

"Oh my goodness!" she whispered to herself,

"could it be that my poor children are still alive?"

They ran home to fetch a pair of scissors, needle and thread. Then the mother cut open the wicked wolf's hairy coat and out popped a little head. One little goat jumped out, followed by another, then another, until all six were set free. Not one of them was hurt, because the greedy monster had swallowed them all whole!

They danced and sang and hugged each other, and their mother said,

"Quickly, go and fetch as many stones as you can find, so we can fill up the wolf's stomach before he wakes up."

They gathered a pile of huge stones, and put them into his stomach. Their mother sewed up the slit with the needle and thread, and all the while, the greedy wolf did not stir. When at last he woke up, he was very thirsty and went to a stream to have a drink. But as he rolled along

from side to side, the stones tumbled about inside his body and he cried out:

> *"What rattles, what rattles*
> *Against my poor bones?*
> *Not little goats, I think,*
> *But only big stones!"*

When the wolf reached the edge of the stream he bent down to take a drink, and the heavy stones made him lose his balance, so that he fell, and sank beneath the water. All the while the little goats and their mother were watching from behind the trees. When they saw the big splash, they came running up, singing, "The wolf is dead! the wolf is dead!" and they danced for joy around their mother by the side of the stream.

# Old Mother Frost

ILLUSTRATED BY STEPHEN ANGEL

There was once a widow who had two daughters. One was beautiful and hard-working. The other was ugly and lazy. The widow was kinder towards the ugly girl, because she was her own daughter, and she made the other one do all the chores.

The poor maiden was forced out every day to sit at the roadside by a well to spin. She spun so much she made her fingers bleed. One day she bled so badly that the spindle became covered in blood, and she tried to wash it in the water in the well. As she leaned over, she accidentally let go and the spindle dropped into the water and sank to the bottom.

The maiden ran crying to her stepmother who scolded her and said, "As you were the one to let the spindle fall into the well, you must go in after it and get it out again."

The poor girl went back to the well in despair and, not knowing what else she could do, jumped right into the well to get the spindle out. As she tumbled, she felt as though she had entered into a dream-like sleep and awoke to find herself

in a beautiful meadow, where the sun was shining, birds were singing and thousands of flowers bloomed all around her.

Before her was a path and she followed it until she came to a baker's where the oven was full of bread. The loaves cried out to her,

"Take me out, take me out, or I shall be burned, for I have been baked long enough." So one by one, she took the loaves out of the oven.

The maiden walked on further, until she came to an apple tree laden with ripe fruit which called out to her, "Shake us, shake us, for we are all ripe!" So she shook the tree until they had all fallen, and then she gathered them into a great heap and continued on her path.

At last she reached a cottage, and at the window she could see an old woman looking out at her. She had very large teeth, and the girl was so frightened at the sight of her, she turned tail and ran. But the old woman called out to her,

"Do not be afraid, child, but come and stay with me, and put my house in order. All things will go well for you, as long as you make my bed properly, and shake it well so that all the feathers fly. Then it will snow upon the earth, for I am Old Mother Frost."

The old woman had such a kind voice, that the maiden took courage, and agreed to stay with her and serve her. Every day she shook her bed so that the feathers blew down like flakes of snow, so the girl's life was happy, and the old woman saw to it that she was well fed and cared for.

The girl stayed with the old woman for a long time, but then she started to feel sad. At first she could not tell why she felt so sad, but after a while she knew that it was because she was homesick.

Even though her life here was so much better, she still longed to be back in her own home.

"I would like to go home," she said to her mistress,

"and if it does not go as well with me below as up here, then I will have to return."

"I could tell that you were homesick," said Old Mother Frost,

"and as you have served me so well, when you decide you want to return, I shall bring you back here myself."

She led the maiden to a door in the loft which she unlatched, and when the girl was standing beneath it, a shower of gold fell down on her, and much of it stuck to her.

"This is your reward for all your hard work," said the old woman, handing her the spindle which she had dropped into the well. The door was closed, and immediately the maiden found herself standing outside her old home.

She went in to her stepmother, and because she was covered in gold, she was not scolded for her long absence. The maiden told her story, and when the stepmother heard how she had come to possess all this gold, she decided to send her lazy, ugly daughter to try her luck.

So she told the girl to sit beside the well and spin. The lazy girl pricked her finger on a thorn to mark the spindle with her blood, dropped it into the well and dived in. She found herself in the same beautiful meadow and followed the same path.

When she came upon the baker's and heard the bread calling out,

"Take me out, take me out, or I shall be burned, for I have been baked long enough," she replied,

"I'm not going to dirty my hands to help you."

When she came to the apple tree laden with ripe fruit which called out to her, "Shake us, shake us, for we are all ripe!" she said,

"Why don't you just fall and let me catch one of you?"

She continued along the path until she came to Old Mother Frost's cottage. She was not afraid when she saw the teeth, as she had been warned, and she soon agreed to serve the old woman. Thinking of the gold that she would earn, the girl worked hard and well on the first day. But on the second she began to idle; on the third, even more so; until she would not get out of bed in the mornings. She did not make the beds as she should have, so the feathers did not fly.

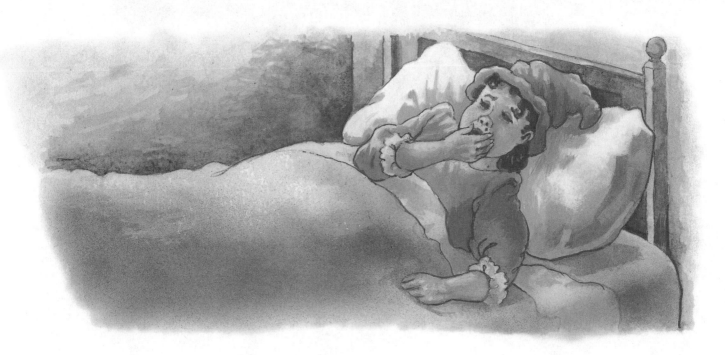

The old woman dismissed the lazy girl from her service, and as she led her to the door, the girl grew very excited, thinking, "Now the gold shower will come." But when she stood under the door, instead of gold, there came upon her a shower of tar. "That is your reward for your service," said the old woman, and shut the door.

The lazy girl came home to her mother's house, and she remained covered in tar for as long as she lived.

# The King's New Clothes

ILLUSTRATED BY JAN NESBITT

Many years ago there lived a King who was very rich and liked nothing more than buying new clothes. He did not enjoy hunting, or going to the theatre, except that these occasions gave him the chance to

71

show off his latest outfits. Time passed away merrily in the town where the King had his castle home, and every day people visited his court. One day two men, calling themselves weavers, asked to see the King.

They told him how they knew how to weave materials of the most beautiful colours and patterns, and how the clothes made from these materials were invisible to all who were unfit for the office they held, as well as to those who were exceptionally stupid.

"These must be splendid clothes," thought the King to himself, "and it will be useful to know who in my kingdom is wise, and who is stupid, and who is unfit for the office they hold."

"Yes, make me a fine suit of clothes from this fabric," said the King, and he ordered a large sum of money to be given to the two men, so that they might start work at once.

The rogues asked to be supplied with vast quantities of the finest silk and gold thread, which they hid in the cellars of their

houses. Then they set up a workshop with two looms, and pretended to work at weaving the amazing cloth.

Everyone in the city heard about the suit of clothes that was being made for the King, and they were all anxious to learn how wise, or indeed how foolish, their neighbours would turn out to be. Not to mention who would be found to be unfit for the office they held.

"I should like to know how the weavers are getting on with my cloth," thought the King one day.

But he was a little nervous about going to have a look himself, for he thought it possible that he might be found to be stupid, or unfit to be King.

So he decided to send his faithful old minister, "for he is a man of good sense, and if anyone is fit for his office, it is he," said the King.

So the faithful old minister went to see the weavers, and found them working away at the empty looms.

"What does this mean?" he said to himself, for he could see no fabric.

"Could it be that I am stupid, or even not fit for my office? I must pretend that I can see it."

"Come closer," said one of the knaves, and look at the pattern. Is it not beautiful?"

"Yes," replied the old minister, "it is excellent. I will tell his Majesty today just how beautiful it is."

They talked at length about the pattern and the colours, and the minister listened carefully to every word so he could tell the King exactly what it looked like.

Then the two men asked for more silk and gold thread to be brought to them, so they could finish making the fabric. They hid these in the cellars of their houses, and continued to pretend to work at the empty looms.

74

A few days later, the King sent another of his officers to see when the cloth would be ready. When he saw the empty looms he also decided to pretend that he could see the cloth, not wanting anyone to know that he was either stupid, or not fit to hold his profitable office.

So when the two men asked him,

"Are you not delighted with the colours and the pattern?" he replied,

"Yes, it is very beautiful," and he too listened carefully to their descriptions. He returned to the King with a detailed account of the fabric.

Soon the whole city was talking about the remarkable cloth that was being woven especially for the King. And now the King himself decided to go and examine it.

He selected a number of courtiers to accompany him, including the two who had already admired the cloth. The men appeared to be working hard at the empty looms as the royal party entered the room. The two officers, imagining everyone else could see the fabric on the loom, declared,

"Look at these patterns, look at these colours; is it not magnificent?"

"Oh dear," thought the King, "how can this be? I can see nothing. I cannot let anyone think that I am a fool, or that I am unfit to be King."

So he said, "It is amazing! I must have a suit of clothes made from this fabric to wear for the procession."

And all his courtiers applauded this decision, even though not one of them could see anything at all.

It was not many days before the grand royal procession

was due to take place in the city, and the tricksters sat up late every night, pretending to cut and pin and sew.

"Look!" they cried at last, "the King's new clothes are ready."

The courtiers gathered to escort the King to the chamber where the rogues were waiting to dress him in his new suit. As he entered, they raised their arms as if they were holding something up, saying,

"Here is your coat, your Majesty," and "Here are your trousers. This is the shirt, and these are the fine undergarments you will need to put on. The whole suit is so light that when you wear it you will feel as though you are wearing nothing at all! "

Not one of the courtiers could see a thing, yet they all declared how exquisite the garments appeared.

"If your Majesty will be pleased to take  off your clothes, we will fit your new suit."

The King

was undressed by his personal servants and stood in front of a mirror while the two rogues pretended to

put on the new suit.

"How splendid his Majesty looks," cried out the courtiers, "and how well the clothes fit,"

"The colours are beautiful," said one,

"the design is magnificent,"said another, as the King

turned from side to side, admiring himself in the mirror. Out in the streets all the people were talking about the King's amazing new suit. There was great excitement as they took their places, wondering who would be found to be wise and who among them were fools.

Meanwhile, at the palace, the King smoothed down his imaginary coat and his courtiers busied themselves

arranging the train on the floor behind him.

Then six of them pretended to pick it up and walked proudly behind the King. A crown was placed on his head, and he set off on his grand procession through the streets.

The people gasped as they saw him approach, and cried out,

"Your clothes are beautiful!"
Not one of them could see a stitch on the King, but they did not want to appear foolish in front of the King or their fellow citizens.

Those who held office, high and low, were mindful of losing their positions in life, so they were not willing to confess to what they really saw.

But there was a little boy in the crowd who had not heard the story about the King's magic suit of clothes, and as the grand procession came into view, the child let out a piercing shriek and cried, "Look at the King! Look at the King!

The King has got no clothes on!"

Another voice was heard to say, "The King has got no clothes on!"

And then another, and another until the whole town was filled with laughter as they all realised that they had been tricked.

Everyone except the King and his officers was laughing. The poor man walked on in a most dignified manner, with those following holding up the imaginary train until they reached the safety of the palace.

What became of the two tricksters? Well, the instant that the King and his party had left the palace, they raced home, emptied the cellar of their treasure and loaded it onto a cart. By the time the grand procession was over they had escaped into another kingdom, and they lived there in the lap of luxury for the rest of their days.

# Rapunzel

ILLUSTRATED BY DAVID LONG

Once upon a time there lived a man and his wife who wished for a child, but many years passed, and they were disappointed. From the window of their house they could see a beautiful garden full of flowers and vegetables. It was surrounded by a high wall and no one dared enter there, for it belonged to a Witch whom everyone feared.

One day the woman was looking out of her window and saw a bed of beautiful radishes which she longed to eat. The longing was so great that as the days passed, she became sick for wanting them. Her husband asked her,

"Why are you sick?"

"I fear that I shall die," she replied softly, "if I do not eat some of those beautiful radishes that I see when I look out of my window."

The poor man thought "I do not want my wife to die, so I must get her what she longs for."

He waited until it was dark, and climbed over the wall into the

Witch's garden. It was quite deserted, and he escaped with a bag full of luscious radishes.

They were such a lovely flavour that the woman wanted more, so the next evening her husband waited until it was dark, and climbed over the wall into the wicked Witch's garden.

As he landed on the grass, there was the Witch in front of him.

"You thief! Come to steal some more of my radishes have you? Evil will come upon you for this!"

"Please have mercy," begged the man, "I only did this for my wife, for I feared she would die if she did not eat the radishes she saw from her window."

"In that case," said the Witch, "go and help yourself to all the radishes you want, but there will be a price to pay. When you have a child you must give it to me. I will take care of it and treat it as a mother would."

The poor man was so frightened that he consented. A year later his wife gave birth to a baby girl and the Witch gave her the name "Rapunzel" and took her away.

Rapunzel grew to be the most beautiful child under the sun, and when she was twelve years old the Witch locked her up in a tower.

This tower stood in the middle of a forest, and had no door, and no stairs. When the Witch wanted to enter the tower, she called up to the window:

*"Rapunzel! Rapunzel!*
*Let down your hair."*

Rapunzel had very long and beautiful hair, as fine as spun gold. When she heard the Witch's voice, she opened the window and let her hair fall down to the ground, and the Witch climbed up the hair to the top.

Three or four years passed and it happened that the King's son was riding through the forest. As he came close to the tower he heard the sound of a beautiful voice singing, and he looked up to see

Rapunzel at her window. The Prince wanted to reach her, but he saw that the tower had no door. So he went home feeling very sad.

Rapunzel's singing had so enchanted the Prince that he rode out to the tower every day just to listen to her. One day he saw the Witch come and call:

"Rapunzel! Rapunzel!
Let down your hair."

The Prince watched as Rapunzel's hair fell to the ground and the Witch climbed up.

"So that is how I must reach her. I will try tomorrow."

The Prince returned to the tower the next day and when Rapunzel finished singing he called out:

*"Rapunzel! Rapunzel!*
*Let down your hair."*

Her tresses fell down and the Prince climbed up. At first Rapunzel was frightened at the sight of a man, for she had never seen one before, but the Prince was so kind and gentle that she soon lost her terror.

He asked her if she would be willing to marry him. The Prince was very handsome, and Rapunzel was longing to be set free from the Witch and her lonely life in the tower.

"I would go with you anywhere but I have no way of climbing down from here. Each time you come to me, bring me silk to weave into a ladder, so I can escape."

The Prince visited Rapunzel every evening because the Witch always came in the day, and they kept their secret safe from the old woman.

Then one day Rapunzel said to her,

"How is it that you find it so hard to climb up to me, when the King's son is with me in a moment?"

The Witch was furious. "I thought I had separated you from the world, and now you have deceived me, you wicked child!"

She took a pair of scissors and cut off Rapunzel's beautiful golden hair.

The Witch tied the tresses to the window latch and took poor Rapunzel to a desert where she left her to die.

The Witch returned to the tower later that

day and waited for the Prince to come. When he called out:

*"Rapunzel! Rapunzel!*
*Let down your hair."*

She let down the
tresses, he climbed up and
into the window, but
instead of Rapunzel, he
found himself face to face
with the Witch.

"Aha!" she exclaimed,
"your beautiful bird no
longer sits in her nest,
singing.

The cat has taken her away and will now scratch out your eyes.
You will never see Rapunzel again."

The poor Prince was so
unhappy that he leapt out
of the window of the tower.
He fell into a bush, which
saved him from death, but
the thorns put out his eyes,
and he wandered blind, in

the forest. He wandered like this for two years, until one day, he heard a voice, which he thought he knew, softly singing. As he approached, Rapunzel recognised him and fell on his neck. Her tears washed over the Prince's eyes and he could see again.

Together they travelled to his kingdom where they were greeted with much rejoicing, and where they lived long and happy lives.

What became of the old Witch no one ever knew.